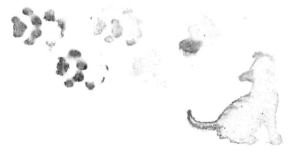

From the Books of

Alexis Jacobson

The Four Little Kittens Storybook

By Kathleen N. Daly
Illustrated by Lilian Obligado

A Golden Book • New York
Western Publishing Company, Inc., Racine, Wisconsin 53404

For Lucille Ogle and Ole Risom,
friends and mentors to both of us:
With love and thanks,
Kathleen and Lilian

Contents

The Four Little Kittens

Once upon a time, four kittens were born in a corner of a barn.

"I wonder what kind of cats they'll grow up to be," thought the mother cat.

She licked her four new babies proudly. They were still tiny. Their eyes were sealed shut, and they could only mew, and snuggle close to their mother's warm side.

In a few days, the kittens opened their eyes. Each day they grew a little bigger, and a little stronger. "And a great deal naughtier," thought Mother Cat, as they pounced on her twitchy tail.

"Children," she said one day, "the time has come for you to decide what kind of cats you will be."

"Tell us, tell us," mewed the kittens, "what kinds of cats there are."

Mother Cat sat up straight, and half closed her green eyes, and began.

"There are Alley Cats.

"An Alley Cat is long and lean. He slinks like a shadow, sleeps where he can, eats what he finds.

"A free cat is he—no manners to mind, no washing of paws, no sheathing of claws. He does what he likes, and nobody knows but he.

"Your Uncle Tom is an Alley Cat. Many friends he has, and they make fine music at night, to the moon.

"His enemies are stray dogs, and turning wheels, and cold, sleety rain. He's a wild and clever cat, the Alley Cat."

"That is the life for me," said Tuff, the biggest kitten. And off he went, to be an Alley Cat, like bold Uncle Tom.

"Now Uncle Tar was a Ship's Cat," Mother Cat went on.
"A splendid cat he was, with a ship for a home,
and sailors for friends.

"A Ship's Cat visits seaports a thousand miles away,
and talks to foreign cats, and chases foreign rats
that try to come aboard.

"A brave cat he is, a jolly, roving cat, a Ship's Cat.
And many are the tales your Uncle Tar could tell."

"That is the life for me," said Luff, the second kitten.
And off he went, to be a Ship's Cat, like jolly Uncle Tar.

"And of course," said Mother Cat, "there are Farm Cats.

"I am a Farm Cat, a useful cat. I catch the mice and chase the rats,
while the farmer sleeps at night.

"I live in the barn on a bed of straw—no House Cat am I.

"A Farm Cat can talk to all the animals that live on the farm.

"A splendid, useful, strong cat is the Farm Cat—
though I say it myself."

"That is the life for me," said Ruff, the third kitten.
And off he went, to be a Farm Cat, like his mother.
Mother Cat purred.

Now the smallest, youngest kitten was called Muff.
Muff was gentle, and playful, and pretty, and always
kept her white paws clean.

Muff's mother sighed and said, "Muff, I don't think you are
an Alley Cat. I don't think you are a Ship's Cat, or even a Farm Cat.
I don't know what kind of cat you are."

And off went Mother Cat, to catch a nice, fat mouse for dinner.

Sadly, Muff wandered out of the barn.

She caught sight of Ruff, getting ready to spring on a great big rat.
Muff shivered, and crept by as quietly as she could.

"I couldn't be a Farm Cat," said Muff, "because I'm *afraid*
of big rats."

Muff wandered out of the farm and down to the village.

She saw plump little Tuff, doing his best to look lean and wild
like an Alley Cat.

"Wuff, wuff," barked a little stray dog, and Tuff arched his back,
and bristled his fur, and spat and hissed in his best Alley Cat way.

The little dog ran away. And so did Muff.

Down to the river she ran, and she saw Luff on a big ship
in the harbor.

The sailors were busy with ropes and things, but already
Luff had curled up in a place where he wouldn't be in the way.
Soon Luff would be visiting cats a thousand miles away,
just like Uncle Tar.

Muff waved good-by. "I wish I knew what kind of cat *I* am,"
she sighed. Then she had to run out of the way as a bicycle
came by.

It began to rain, and Muff got cold and wet. She didn't like that
at all, and she shook her wet paws crossly. She lay down to sleep
on a lumpy pile of sacks. She didn't like that very much, either.

She was cold and hungry and cross, and when a big hand
picked her up, she spat and hissed for all the world like an Alley Cat.

But the big hand put her into a big, warm pocket, and after
a few more angry squawks, and a sad little mew, Muff fell asleep.

When next she opened her eyes, Muff was in a house. There were cushions and carpets and curtains. There was a warm, crackling fire.

There was a little girl with soft, gentle hands.

"Oh, what a lovely kitten," said the little girl. "Oh, I wanted a kitten so much. Now I won't be lonely any more."

The little girl gave Muff a saucer of cream. Muff drank it all, with one white foot in the saucer to keep it steady. Then she washed her paw, and licked her whiskers.

This was *much* better than fat mice for dinner.

The little girl played with Muff. She dangled a string, and Muff jumped and pounced in her prettiest way, and the little girl laughed with delight.

Muff purred.

This was much better than running away from barking dogs and turning wheels.

The little girl lifted Muff onto her warm lap, and stroked Muff's fur.

"Oh, it's nice to have a kitten," said the little girl happily.

Muff purred loudly.

This was much better than a pile of lumpy sacks, or even a bed of straw.

"This is the life for me," purred Muff. "I know what kind of cat I am, at last.

"I'm a cushion and cream cat, a purring cat, a cuddlesome cat, a playful cat, a little girl's cat—I'm a House Cat!"

And so all four kittens lived happily ever after—Tuff in his alley,
because he was an Alley Cat, Ruff on his farm, because he was
a Farm Cat, Luff on his ship. because he was a Ship's Cat,
and Muff on her cushions, in her house, with her little girl, because
she was a House Cat.

Muff, the House Cat

Muff soon found out that being a House Cat meant
that she had lots of important things to do.

For one thing, she had to keep her little girl warm on cold winter
days. Muff curled up in the little girl's lap and purred softly
while the little girl read books and painted pictures.

At night, Muff slept near the little girl's feet to keep them cozy.

Sometimes Muff had to chase away small mice, and even catch one
or two. She always brought the dead mouse to the little girl,
and the girl said, "Thanks for the present," very politely.

As the little girl grew up, Muff helped her with her homework.
Muff tapped on the typewriter and made paw prints on the paper.

The girl said, "Thank you, Muff."

When the girl had piano practice, Muff tried to help with her paws.
The girl laughed and laughed, and hugged Muff. The piano teacher
didn't laugh so much.

Muff always kept her paws and face and whiskers clean and shiny.

"You are a good House Cat," said the girl.

But one day the girl went away, and she didn't come back that night, or the next day, or the next.

Muff meowed and fretted.

"She's gone away to school, Muff," said the girl's parents.

Muff felt very lonely. Perhaps, she thought, she had made the wrong choice, after all. Perhaps being a House Cat wasn't right for her. She had to find out.

She wondered what her brothers, Tuff, Luff, and Ruff, were doing. Muff set off on a journey to find her brothers.

Muff found the farm where Ruff lived. A big black-and-white sheepdog barked at Muff. The cows mooed at her. And the geese hissed.

But Ruff gave her a brotherly kiss and said, "Come and meet my friend, Shadow."

Muff stepped daintily along the path leading to the stables. She stayed very close to Ruff, wondering what a Shadow was.

Muff quickly found out that Shadow was a racehorse—a very large racehorse.

Shadow was delighted to see the little cat. He wanted to lick Muff all over. But Muff was scared of Shadow's big tongue and hooves. She backed away and said to her brother, "I like your friend. He is beautiful. But he's far too big for me. Everything's too big for me around here."

"That's how I used to feel," said Ruff, and he told Muff the story of his first days on the farm.

Muff was still frightened. "I'll say good-by for now," she said.

Muff left in a hurry.

Next Muff went to the seaport where she had last seen Luff.

"Luff isn't in port right now," said a friendly sailor cat. "He's traveling on ships and boats all over the world. He's a very brave sailor cat."

"Just like his Uncle Tar," said Muff.

"I'll tell you all about him," said the sailor cat, who loved to tell stories.

Muff sat down to listen while the sailor cat spun his yarn about Luff.

"Goodness," said Muff, when he had finished. "He really is a brave cat. *I* could never be so daring. So I'll say good-by for now, Sailor Cat. Give Luff my love!"

Then she set off to the city, to look for Tuff.

And pretty soon she saw a big red fire engine screeching by,
with Tuff and some other cats aboard.

Muff followed the engine to Firehouse Number Seven.

And what a fuss there was when Tuff saw his sister!

"Come and meet Delicat and the kittens!" he said.

Tuff told the story of how he had met Delicat, and a wonderful
story it was. Muff was very proud of her brother, the hero. She liked
the beautiful Delicat. But most of all, she liked the kittens.
There were four of them, each one spotted black and white.

"Stay with us, stay with us, Auntie Muff," said the kittens.
"We have such fun at the Firehouse and in the Alley!"

"I love you, dears," said Muff, "but all of a sudden, I know what
I must do. I must go to my house and be a House Cat and make
new kittens. Then I can tell them the stories of their brave and
splendid uncles."

And Muff hurried home.

There she found her little girl. She was quite grown up now, but she was crying.

Muff quickly sprang into her lap and rubbed against her face.

"Oh, Muff! I thought you had gone away forever," said the girl. "I felt so very sad. Please, please, don't go away again!"

Muff purred her best purr, and said, "Meow!" She meant, "I'll never go away again, because now I know for sure that I'm a cushion and cream cat, a cuddlesome cat, a playful cat, a girl's cat— I'm a House Cat!"

Soon Muff had four little kittens of her own. She purred with happiness as the girl petted them.

When the kittens got bigger, she told them the stories of Ruff, Tuff, and Luff, and she told them about herself.

"A House Cat I was meant to be, and that is what I am," she said, "and I am well content."

Now listen to the stories that Muff told about her brothers.

Ruff, the Farm Cat

"Ruff was born and brought up on the farm. Our mother was a Farm Cat," said Muff. "She taught Ruff everything she knew about the farm."

But still, life started out to be difficult for Ruff. He was a small cat—and everywhere he went, he found animals that were much bigger than he was.

Trim, the black-and-white sheepdog, was very polite, and he was nice to Ruff. But Trim could bark very loudly, and sometimes Ruff got scared and ran away.

Then there were the cows. They were enormous. Ruff enjoyed their milk. But he was scared of their big, clumsy feet.

Even the white geese were much bigger than Ruff, and bad-tempered, too. When Ruff got too close to their babies, the mother geese rushed at him, hissing angrily, and Ruff ran for his life.

Ruff did what he could to help on the farm. He chased the mice and killed the rats, which were much smaller than he was. He kept himself neat and clean. His fur shone and his sharp claws glistened.

But, "Oh dear," thought Ruff, "it's awful to be small and scared!"

One day there was a big fuss at the farm. The farmer cleaned out the old horse stable—Ruff's favorite hiding place. He made it spick-and-span, and put in some fresh straw.

Then some men arrived with a trailer behind their car.

And out of the trailer stepped a beautiful racehorse called Shadow.

When the groom tried to lead Shadow into the stable, a big white goose ran by. The horse sidestepped, his ears laid back and his eyes rolling.

"This is one very nervous horse," said the groom. "He got a terrible fright with his last owner, and he just won't calm down. It's impossible to race him right now."

"A few weeks in my nice, quiet stable will help him," said the farmer.

Ruff watched as the farmer stroked and patted the nervous horse and finally got him into the stable.

"Why, that horse is very beautiful and very, very big, and yet he's even more scared than I am!" thought Ruff.

When everyone had gone away, Ruff crept down from the rafters and went close to the horse. He meowed softly, and the horse stared at him with big eyes.

Then Ruff sat down and began to wash himself, calm as you please.

Shadow lowered his big head and sniffed softly at the cat.

Then Ruff started to rub himself against those tall legs, purring loudly. He was saying to the horse, "Hello, Horse. I know you feel scared. I'm your friend. Now just you calm down!"

And there was something about that small, purring cat that made Shadow feel peaceful. After a few days, he even let Ruff curl up on his broad back and go to sleep. When the groom saw the cat on Shadow's back, he shooed Ruff away. Then Shadow snorted in fear, dancing nervously and swishing his tail.

"We'd better get that cat back," said the farmer, who knew a thing or two about horses.

So they found Ruff, and sure enough, the horse calmed down again. He licked that little cat with his big tongue, enough to flatten him down, but Ruff didn't mind, and the farmer chuckled.

"It's a funny thing about horses," he said. "Sometimes they really seem to need the company of small creatures like Ruff."

From that day on, Ruff stayed with the horse all the time.

When Shadow was ready to race again, Ruff went first into
the trailer, and Shadow followed happily.

At the racetrack, Ruff purred into Shadow's ear, and the horse felt
so good that he ran the race faster than any of the other horses, just so
he could get back to his little friend. And Shadow kept winning every
race he ran! His new owner was very pleased.

Ruff drank milk from the silver cups that Shadow won. He rubbed
against Shadow's famous legs. He sat on Shadow's back and purred.
And Shadow was just as calm and happy as could be, and so was Ruff.

One day, Shadow's owner presented Ruff with a small silver cup.
On it was written,

"You don't have to be big to be a champ!"

Ruff purred and said to Shadow, "That's what I'm going to tell
my little kittens, someday."

Tuff, the Alley Cat

"Tuff was King of the Alley, there was no doubt about that," said Muff.

Even the bravest dogs put their tails behind their legs and fled at the sight of him.

The policeman on the beat grinned and tipped his hat at Tuff as he walked by.

Big John, the fire chief, honked his horn and waved at Tuff.

Shopkeepers put out scraps of food for Tuff and invited him to come inside.

Tuff knew every person, and every doorway, and every corner in the Alley.

The other Alley Cats watched their manners when Tuff was around. All of them had worse scars than those on Tuff's sleek black coat.

Yes, Tuff was King of the Alley, all right, lean and long and strong.

One fine summer evening, as the sun was sinking behind
the big water towers on the rooftops, Tuff woke up from his
afternoon nap.

He gave a big yawn, showing his large pink mouth and sharp teeth.
The other cats shivered. Mice and rats ran for their lives. Pigeons flew
up to the rooftops.

Tuff stretched his back and his legs.

Then he started off down the Alley, slow and lazy looking,
but his eyes and nose and whiskers didn't miss a thing.

Mr. Baits, the fish man, put out a saucer of scraps. Tuff
sniffed at the fish and gave a small purr as Mr. Baits scratched
behind Tuff's ears.

Then Tuff moved on, leaving some scraps on the plate. He always
did that, just to show that he didn't *really* need the food. He had only
dropped in to say a polite hello.

Mrs. Muldoon was sitting on her stoop with the other ladies,
enjoying the sunset and the gossip.

"Here, Kitty-Kitty!" said Mrs. Muldoon.

Tuff pretended not to hear. He *hated* being called Kitty.
Didn't she know that by now?

"Wuff, wuff!" barked a fat puppy. He ran at Tuff, who arched
his back and growled. The puppy stopped and stared, wagging
his tail.

Then the puppy came closer. Tuff batted his nose with a paw and needle-sharp claws. The puppy turned tail and ran, terrified.

Tuff sat down and licked his paw, feeling pleased with himself.

"You may think you're brave, but I think that was pretty mean. He was just a friendly puppy," said a cool cat voice.

Tuff stared in astonishment. The voice belonged to the most beautiful cat he had ever seen. Her coat was creamy white, her eyes were blue, and her nose was pink.

"How do you do?" said Tuff. "You must be new on the Alley. I'm tough, and Tuff is my name."

"There's nothing tough about scaring a puppy," said the white cat. She flicked her tail at Tuff and turned to leave. "My name is Delicat, and this deli is where I plan to live. I like pickles. Good night, Tuff-Cat."

Tuff stalked off, his feelings hurt. Nobody talked to him like that in the Alley. What did she mean, he wasn't tough?

He chased two large dogs, and killed a rat to put on Mrs. Muldoon's doorstep. He darted at the wheels of a bicycle, and the rider fell off. Tuff felt better, but he couldn't stop thinking about the beautiful Delicat.

The sun rose at the east end of the Alley, over Firehouse Number Seven. Tuff yawned and curled up in the doorway of Ida's Ice Cream Parlor. He knew that later he would get a cool lunchtime snack from Ida, and he fell asleep happy.

That evening Tuff shined his coat and claws and whiskers till they glistened. Then he set off on his rounds, slow and lazy looking, lean and long and strong.

But there were no fish scraps that night. Mr. Baits had gone to the Palace Movie House. And Mrs. Muldoon and her friends stayed indoors, since it looked like rain. In fact, the Alley was very quiet that night. Tuff felt lonely.

Tuff sat down to lick his paws and face. Suddenly his nose twitched and he smelled an awful smell. Smoke! Smoke was pouring out of the delicatessen.

Tuff hated bad smells. He was about to walk off when he heard a voice.

"Help, Tuff-Cat! It's me, Deli! The place is on fire! Please help me!"

Tuff raced to the delicatessen. He saw Delicat in the window, running back and forth between the pickles and the salami and the sausages.

Black smoke was pouring out of the vent above the closed door. There was no sign of Dan, the deli man. The fire alarm was clanging. Tuff thought fast.

"Quick, this way!" said Tuff.

Tuff raced around the corner to the back entrance
of the delicatessen. He knew very well that there was a small hole
in the basement window at the back. He had made it himself,
the night he had chased a very large rat out of the cellar.

He found the hole and put his head inside it and yowled.

Delicat stumbled through the smoke toward the sound of Tuff's
loud meow. She found the hole and scrambled through it.

Tuff licked her sooty face.

"Oh, Tuff, you saved my life," said Delicat. "You are a brave and
wonderful cat!"

She licked his face.

Tuff purred.

Just then the fire engine came. The fire fighters put out the fire
in no time.

Mr. Baits, and Mrs. Muldoon and her friends, and Dan the deli man, and all the neighbors gathered around.

Then Big John, the fire chief, put Tuff under one arm and Delicat under the other. "I think you two brave cats belong in the Firehouse," he said, and everyone agreed.

And that is how Tuff and Delicat became Firehouse Cats. To this day, you can see them, and their black-and-white-spotted kittens, riding the fire engine. The kittens look a little like firehouse dogs, only better, because they are cats.

Tuff is still King of the Alley, and Delicat is Queen. But she doesn't like pickles any more.

Luff, the Ship's Cat

"Now my brother Luff began his life on a small fishing boat, just like his Uncle Tar," said Muff.

He liked the fishermen, and he liked the seagulls, and most of all he liked the food. There was fish for breakfast, fish for lunch, fish for dinner, and fish for snacks in between.

But just like any sailor, Luff liked a change of scene every once in a while. So Luff jumped off the fishing boat when they got back to port.

He sat on the dockside, washing his face and whiskers and paws, and looking at the ships and the sailors nearby. And pretty soon, Luff went aboard a big oil tanker. The ship carried oil to places far across the seas.

One day the oiler went into port at a beautiful tropical island. Luff went ashore to stretch his legs and to meet some very large birds called pelicans. And the oiler left without him.

"Well, that's a sailor's life," said Luff.

He sat on the dockside, washing his face and whiskers and paws, and looking at the ships and sailors nearby. Then he saw a small boat.

It was unloading a cargo of bananas and coconuts, bicycles, spare parts for cars, toilet bowls, and kitchen sinks.

"I think I'll take that ship," said Luff.

He strolled aboard and quickly found his way to the galley.
"Meow," he said politely.

The young cook said, "Oh boy, a cat! Welcome aboard, Cat.
This is my first trip away from home. I need a friend!"

The boy gave him a big bowl of scraps, and Luff purred a lot.

At night, Luff slept on the boy's bunk. He felt very happy,
and so did the boy.

Then one night the boat got caught in a terrible storm—it was
a howling hurricane! Enormous waves crashed down on the little
boat, and the boat rolled and pitched and yawed.

The boy felt very seasick. He got out of his bunk and went up
on deck. But the boat was rolling so much that the boy slipped and
hit his head. He fell down, and there he lay, close to the rail and
the mighty waves.

Luff hated the storm. He tried to hide under the pillow, and then
under the bunk. Then he decided that maybe topside would be better.

He climbed up the steps. And he saw the boy lying still as still on the deck.

"Meow," said Luff. But the boy didn't answer.

Luff licked his face. No answer.

A wave broke on the deck, and Luff clung to the boy.

Now Luff was soaked with salt water, and he didn't like it at all.

He decided to go to the captain's bridge to dry off. But he was also worried about the boy. Why was the boy asleep on the deck, all salty and wet? Didn't he know he could get washed away by the waves?

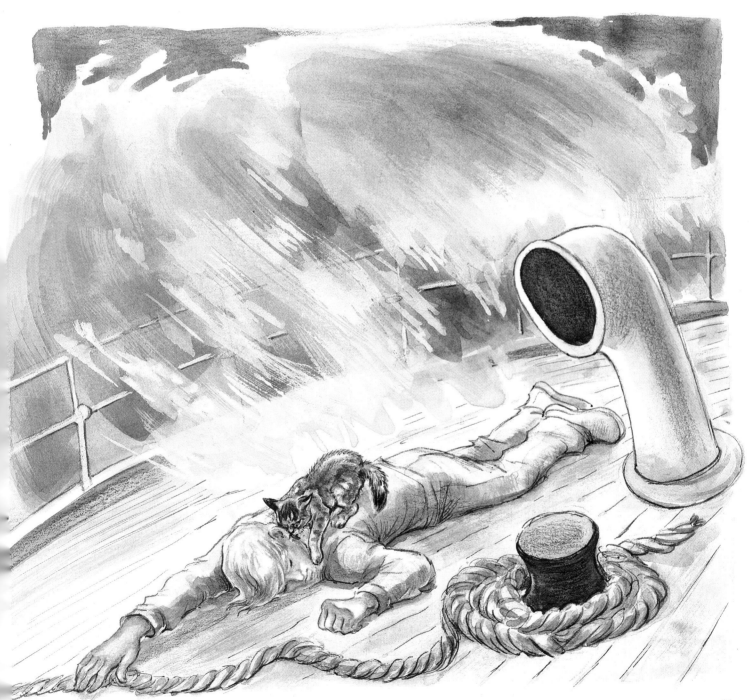

Luff went up to the bridge, meowing all the way.

The captain patted Luff's head and said, "Nasty storm, Cat."

Luff said, "Me-OW!" He meant, "The boy is in danger and you'd better do something about it." But of course the captain, being human, didn't understand cat-talk, and he said, "There, there, Cat."

Luff went to the stairs and said, "Me-OW!" very loudly.

But the captain didn't hear him, so Luff pounced on the captain's leg and dug in his sharp claws and yowled.

"Ouch," said the captain. "What's the matter, Cat?"

"I think he's trying to tell us something," said the mate, who was the captain's helper.

The mate followed Luff down the stairs, and he saw the boy.

A huge wave crashed down, and the boy and the mate and the cat all got very wet. But they held on to each other, and nobody was swept overboard.

Pretty soon they were all safe and dry in their bunks, and the captain tucked them in and gave them some hot cocoa.

The next day, the captain said to the boy, "That cat saved your life, my boy."

"Yes, sir," said the boy.

"But he ruined my sock," said the captain. He held up the sock for all to see. "Keep this sock, young man," he said to the cook. "It will remind you to be more careful when you move around on a boat."

"And it will remind me of a brave and clever cat," said the boy.

Luff said nothing. He was too busy washing the salt from his coat and thinking, "This is a sailor's life. This is the life for me! I wonder what will happen next."

Muff's Four Little Kittens

Muff licked her kittens, and then she yawned.

"It's time to sleep now," she said. "Perhaps you'll dream about what kind of cats you'll be when you grow up."

"Mew, mew," said the four little kittens sleepily.

Muff purred and stretched. She left the sleeping kittens safe in their basket. Then she began to walk quietly around the house, to make sure there were no mice or rats around.

Muff was a good House Cat, and happy in her work.

And she knew that whatever they chose to do, her four little kittens would grow up to be the four best cats ever.